Funky Phantoms

The Ghosts of CREAKIE HALL in Funky Phantoms

Karen Wallace
and Tony Ross

To John 'n' Annie

CATNIP BOOKS
Published by Catnip Publishing Ltd
14 Greville Street
London EC1N 8SB

This edition first published 2011

First published by Puffin Books 1998
1 3 5 7 9 10 8 6 4 2

Text copyright © Karen Wallace, 1998
Illustrations copyright © Tony Ross, 1998
The moral rights of the author and illustrator have
been asserted

A CIP catalogue record for this book is available from
the British Library.

ISBN 978-1-84647-126-1

Printed in Poland

www.catnippublishing.co.uk

CHAPTER 1

MIASMA BOGEY-MANDEVILLE's silver face looked almost see-through in the pale light that lit the attic window at Creakie Hall. She twisted her knee-length orange hair into a soft knot at the back of her head and stared out at her favourite view.

Winter was coming to Creakie Hall. The murky water of Bullfrog Lake shone with a dull metal gleam. Around the edge, frozen bulrushes were stiff and broken, their long stalky stems glittering with frost. Even the maze, usually so wonderfully dense and green, looked brown and bare. It was still just like a prison, though. Miasma smiled to herself. Imagine trying to escape through those thick thorny branches!

In fact, under the first dusting of snow, everything looked white and dead, which gave Miasma a warm cosy feeling as she picked up the dragonfly wing she was making out of lace.

Lace-making was Miasma's latest hobby. During the long winter months, she and her husband, Marmaduke, liked to learn new things. After all, they had been playing poker since 1665 and, even though they both loved it, things hadn't been the same since Miasma had discovered she could see Marmaduke's cards in the mirror behind him. What she didn't know

was that, for the past 399 years, he had been able to see hers in the other mirror. So even though she started to win every game, it was the first time they had ever played on equal terms.

Not that Marmaduke would ever have admitted it. Indeed, Miasma wouldn't have minded. That was the great thing about being ghosts – what was the point in worrying about things? Especially in their case, when all good things never came to an end.

'What rhymes with *cat*, spooky-pet?' muttered Marmaduke from the other side of the room. Marmaduke sat hunched over his huge oak desk sucking the feather on the end of his pen. He tried again. 'What about, "The cat sat on the Turkish rug"?'

Miasma sighed. While she had taken up lace-making, Marmaduke had taken to writing poetry. This was all very well except that he was completely hopeless at it and kept interrupting her with questions.

Worst of all, he was still only on his first poem! Miasma looked around the room. The things she had made out of lace were everywhere. Every corner was hung with a glittering cobweb. And she'd even taught herself to make black woolly spiders with beady eyes that seemed to follow you round the room.

Miasma put down her dragonfly wing. It was her most ambitious project yet. The dragonfly was going to be six foot long with wings as wide as the room. '*Mat*, bogey-baby,' she said sweetly. 'I'm sure that's the word you want. 'The cat sat on the *mat*.'

'That's it!' cried Marmaduke, grabbing a new piece of paper. 'Spooky-pet, you're a genius!'

'It was your idea in the first place,' murmured Miasma. She paused. 'Will you be writing any more poems, do you think?'

Marmaduke leaned back on his chair. 'I'm not sure,' he said in a serious voice. 'I may need to do more work on this one.'

Miasma smiled indulgently at her husband. 'Of course,' she murmured.

And with that they fell into a

peaceful silence which filled the room like a fine grey mist.

Suddenly Miasma gasped and her lace fell from her lap.

Marmaduke looked up quickly. 'What's the . . .' But he never finished his sentence. He sat bolt upright and his eyes went huge and round in his head.

'Marmaduke,' whispered Miasma. 'Can you feel it?'

'I certainly can,' replied Marmaduke. 'And I don't like it one bit.'

Miasma shivered. It was a nasty fizzy feeling in her bones. And she knew it meant only thing.

Danger was threatening Creakie Hall. And that danger was getting nearer!

'I thought Aunt Gardenia closed the hotel for the winter,' muttered Marmaduke.

Aunt Gardenia lived downstairs with her niece and nephew, Polly and George. She was the oldest surviving Bogey-Mandeville and she had turned Creakie Hall into a hotel so that she could keep it in the family.

'She does,' said Miasma. 'I mean she has. She took down the knitted CREAKIE HALL – OPEN TO EVERYONE banner last week.'

Aunt Gardenia's passion was knitting. Everything that could possibly be knitted was knitted at

Creakie Hall. Even the gardener, Osbert Codseye, had been given a knitted cover for his lawnmower to keep it warm during the winter.

Marmaduke got up from his desk and walked over to the window. The fizzy feeling grew stronger.

'Tell you what,' suggested Marmaduke. 'Why don't I have a

quick fly around and see what I can find?'

'Absolutely not!' cried Miasma, her eyes flashing. 'Don't you remember what happened the last time you did that?'

Miasma rolled her eyes. The whole thing had been a nightmare. Marmaduke had turned himself into a pterodactyl by mistake. The next thing they knew, the entire membership of the Royal Society for the Protection of Birds had camped out on Osbert Codseye's beautifully mowed lawn for two weeks, waiting for another sighting.

The only good thing was that Polly and George had made a fortune selling orange squash and sandwiches, although most of that had gone on new grass seed.

Nevertheless, the whole episode

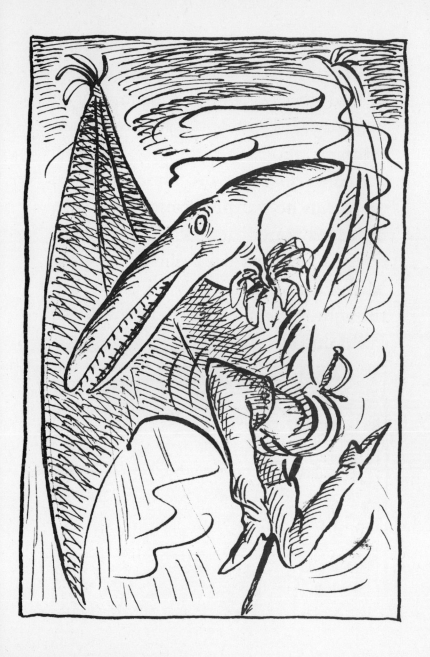

had made Miasma feel horribly *old*.
How could Marmaduke have chosen
a bird that was alive *thousands* of
years ago? What could he have been
thinking of?

It had all been too upsetting and
there was no way Miasma was going
to let it happen again.

'All right, all right,' muttered
Marmaduke, reading her every
thought. 'We'll send Cromwell to
Polly and George.'

Cromwell was the cat and right now Cromwell was asleep on a book on the top shelf of the library. It was his favourite place. And, as it happened, the book was Marmaduke's favourite as a child. It was called *A Boy's Own Blunderbuss.*

Miasma grinned. 'That's a good idea, bogey-baby,' she cried. 'The flesh'n'bloods will know exactly what to do.' She clapped her hands

in excitement. 'Besides, it would be fun to have one more adventure with them before winter comes.'

Above them, Cromwell stretched out one long furry silver paw and, looking up as if by magic, opened one turquoise eye.

'Cromwell,' said Miasma, 'go to Polly and George. They must find out what's going on.'

Cromwell opened both eyes and stretched both furry silver paws. Then slowly, shelf by shelf, he climbed down the front of the library and disappeared through the wall.

CHAPTER 2

UP IN THEIR attic playroom at the other end of the house, Polly and George Bogey-Mandeville were also getting themselves organised for the winter.

They had decided to build a scale model of Creakie Hall Hotel set in its grounds.

'The problem is,' said Polly as she shaped the mould that would become Bullfrog Lake, 'I'm not quite sure what to do about the maze.'

'Why's that?' muttered George through a mouthful of nails. George

was on his hands and knees in a pile
of sawdust, cutting out wooden walls.

'You know there's a well in the
middle of it?' began Polly.

'Mmm.'

'Well, Osbert's going to cover it
over and build a flower bed around
it.'

'Why's that?' muttered George
again.

Polly grinned. 'He thinks the guests should have something pretty to look at while they're waiting.'

'Waiting for what?' said George.

'Waiting to be rescued, of course,' replied Polly. 'You know the maze is just like a prison, George.'

George laughed and went back to his sawing. Winter was one of his favourite times. There was nothing he liked better than to get down to working without being interrupted. And now that Aunt Gardenia had closed the hotel, things would be more peaceful again.

At that moment, an icy breeze fluttered through the room.

Polly and George looked up to see Cromwell walk through the wall.

'Oh dear,' muttered George. 'And there I was thinking how peaceful everything seemed.'

'Funny you should say that,' murmured Polly. 'So was I.' She looked into the cat's unblinking turquoise eyes. 'I wonder what Cromwell's trying to tell us.'

Suddenly, Cromwell shot into the air with all four legs sticking out. He turned a full somersault and landed on the table. Then he lifted

his right paw, pointed his head downwards with his tail held in a straight line behind.

There was no doubt about it. Cromwell wanted Polly and George to go downstairs as quickly as possible.

George dropped his tools. Polly put down her mould of Bullfrog Lake. If Cromwell was here, then something was up. They pulled open the door and ran as fast as they could downstairs.

The front hall was empty. Nothing seemed to have changed. The huge china plant pots on either side of the front door had cosy covers for the winter. The new gold frames around the full-length portraits of Miasma and Marmaduke Bogey-Mandeville glittered in the long mirror opposite.

Only one thing was odd – the door to Aunt Gardenia's study was shut.

Polly and George looked at each other. Aunt Gardenia never shut her door.

Well, not unless she was up to one of her hare-brained schemes to make money for the hotel.

Polly took a deep breath, knocked and opened the door.

'Goodness gracious!' cried Aunt Gardenia, her voice ringing like a tiny silver bell. 'What an extraordinary coincidence. I was just about to call you both!'

Aunt Gardenia looked flushed and excited. In front of her was the big old-fashioned telephone she insisted on using. Beside it, a glossy magazine was open on a page which had the words 'GHOSTS CAN BE GOLD MINES' written across the top.

Two things were immediately obvious to Polly and George – Aunt

Gardenia was about to make or had just made a telephone call and it had something to do with the article in the magazine.

'What was it you wanted to tell us, Aunt Gardenia?' said Polly slowly as she and George sat down on the little flowery sofa opposite their aunt's table.

'It's about this article,' replied Aunt Gardenia, beaming and looking very pleased with herself. 'I'd never even heard of the magazine before it arrived on the doorstep today.'

'Did the postman bring it?' asked George, suspiciously.

'That's the funny thing!' cried Aunt Gardenia. 'It was pushed through the letter box after lunch.' She sat back and smoothed her hair into her bun. 'But good things are *always* unexpected, aren't they, dears?'

Polly picked up the magazine and looked at the article. Nothing in it looked good to her. In fact, the more she read, the further her stomach turned over.

'Isn't it a wonderful idea?' cried Aunt Gardenia. 'Professor Swindel Rattlechain will come with his assistant –' she paused and lifted a finger – 'for free, you'll notice, to see if Creakie Hall has any ghosts.'

'Why would you want to know *that*?' asked George.

Aunt Gardenia beamed. 'Because, dear George, as Professor Rattlechain points out in his article, "Ghosts Can Be Gold Mines". In other words, a hotel with a *nice* class of ghost can be very successful. Guests will come and stay especially to see them.'

'That's all very well,' replied George, 'but how could this Professor Rattlechain and his –' he took the magazine from Polly's knee – 'and his assistant, Scarlet Icepick, possibly find out if there are ghosts in Creakie Hall?'

Aunt Gardenia jumped up from her chair. 'He has a special machine!' she cried. 'It sends out these signals which only ghosts can feel and it draws the ghosts out of their hiding places!'

Polly's stomach turned full circle and felt like a bag of ice cubes inside her. She turned and looked at George. His face was the colour of pale blotting paper.

Polly stared at the telephone on Aunt Gardenia's table. 'Um . . . have you . . . um . . . spoken to anyone about this?' she asked, barely able to get the words out of her mouth.

'Absolutely!' replied Aunt Gardenia. 'I know a good idea when I see one. Professor Rattlechain is on his way right now!'

As she spoke, a strange bullet-shaped van pulled up outside the window. It was painted black with tinted windows so you couldn't see inside it. A metal tower stuck out from the roof, and on top of the tower something that looked like a radar blade was slowly turning round and round.

Polly and George stared at it in horror. No wonder Cromwell had come through the wall to warn them!

There was no time to lose – they had to speak to Marmaduke and Miasma before it was too late.

As Polly and George jumped up from the sofa, the front doors of the bullet-shaped van opened.

From the passenger side, a woman stepped lightly onto the ground. She had crew-cut platinum-blonde hair with a single stripe of scarlet across the top of her head. She was dressed in a black leather jumpsuit covered in silver zippers and popper buttons. Even her boots were black with silver zigzags going up the sides.

Polly stared in disbelief. This woman had to be Scarlet Icepick but Polly had never seen anyone look less likely to be an assistant to a professor.

Then she saw Professor Swindel Rattlechain stride round the front of the van. She watched as he peered up at the spinning blade through square, gold glasses. Professor Rattlechain was dressed in a frock coat with pinstripe trousers. His wavy, white hair looked like ice cream on top of

his head. It also looked like a wig.

Polly let her eyes run back down the pinstripe trousers. There was something peculiar about his shoes. You would have expected black patent slip-ons perhaps or elegant lace-ups. But no – Professor Rattlechain was wearing heavy working boots with steel-capped toes.

'Excellent!' cried Aunt Gardenia. 'Just in time for dinner as well. Come along and meet them, dears!'

'I'll make up their rooms first,' said George, quickly.

'And I'll lay extra places in the dining room,' gasped Polly.

'That's a good idea, dears,' cried Aunt Gardenia. 'What would I do without you?' She sailed into the hall towards the front door. 'Come down when you're ready!'

But Polly and George didn't hear her. They were running as fast as they could up the stairs to the attic.

CHAPTER 3

'POLLY!' CRIED GEORGE as they turned down the long corridor. 'This could be the end of everything. We have to stop that machine from finding Marmaduke and Miasma.'

'I know, I know,' sobbed Polly. 'And *they* must know it too. Why else would they send Cromwell?'

At that moment, the door that only Polly and George knew about appeared in the wall in front of them. It was a heavy, old-fashioned door with a big iron lock.

Just as George put his hand on the

knob, the door swung open.

'Greetings, flesh'n'bloods!' cried Miasma, grinning her wolfish grin. She wrapped her silvery arms around Polly and George's shoulders and led them into the room.

'A not unexpected surprise,' said Marmaduke with a big smile.

Polly and George were stunned. Could it be possible that Marmaduke and Miasma didn't realise how much danger they were in? Or perhaps they were just trying to hide their feelings so as not to upset anyone else.

George took a deep breath. 'No matter what happens, we'll protect you,' he said stoutly.

Miasma clasped her hands and sighed an icy sigh. 'How fiendishly divine of you, darling,' she cried. 'And we'll protect *you*, won't we, Marmaduke?'

'We will, we will!' agreed Marmaduke. 'We'll lay down our . . .' He paused as he remembered that they didn't have any lives to lay down. 'We'll lay down absolutely *everything* else!'

'Look here!' said Polly who was so worried she was almost angry. 'Don't you realise that a Professor Rattlechain has arrived with some horrible ghost-hunting machine to track you down and drag you out of your attic?'

She walked over to the window and pointed at the black bullet-shaped van with the spinning blade. 'Can't you *feel* his machine searching for you?'

Now it was Miasma's turn to look puzzled. 'Searching for *us?*' she said. 'A ghost-hunting machine?' Then she threw back her head and hooted

with laughter. 'There's no such thing
as a ghost-hunting machine.'

'Then why did you send Cromwell
to us?' asked George who was getting

more and more confused. Mind you, this always happened with Marmaduke and Miasma.

'Why?' repeated Miasma. Her eyes blazed like green lightbulbs. 'Why? Because whoever that man is with his nasty-looking butler –'

'The butler's a woman, spooky-pet,' interrupted Marmaduke, who just happened to have read an article about punks the last time he was downstairs. 'It's a kind of fashion called –'

'Well, I'm too old for that kind of fashion,' snapped Miasma. 'And as for that haircut. Nasty, brutish and short.'

'Her name is Scarlet Icepick,' Polly almost shouted. 'Now what were you going to say about Professor Rattlechain?'

'They're fakes,' said Marmaduke in a voice that echoed like a gust of wind in a dungeon. 'We can feel it in our bones.'

'And our bones never lie,' agreed Miasma. 'These people, whoever they are, are a danger to Creakie Hall.'

'But if they're not real ghost hunters,' said George, rubbing his hand over his forehead, 'then we must find out what they're doing here.'

'Exactly, flesh'n'bloods!' cried Miasma, leaping into the air. 'We knew you'd have the answer. That's why we sent for you!'

She paused and gave them another of her wicked grins. 'Also, there's nothing like a bit of fun before a long cold winter, whaddaya say?'

'Miasma,' said Polly sternly, 'this is not a bit of fun. We'll have to make a plan and fast. They're staying the night and by the morning it may be too late!'

At that moment, there was a *poop poop* of a horn from the courtyard below. Everyone looked out of the window.

A really old-fashioned car with no roof and silver-spoked wheels rumbled up to the front door and stopped. A man in goggles and a white scarf jumped out. He was wearing tweed plus fours and a deerstalker hat. In the back seat sat a huge, black

curly-haired dog who was also wearing goggles and a white scarf.

As the man walked round and opened the dog's door, Osbert Codseye came into view.

Imagine Polly and George's surprise when they saw Osbert Codseye's long, mournful face break into a big smile. Imagine their total amazement when they saw Osbert clasp the stranger firmly by the hand and engulf him in a huge bear hug.

Polly and George stared until they thought their eyes might fall out. In all the years they had known him, Osbert Codseye never spoke about friends or family. In fact, Osbert Codseye hardly ever spoke at all.

'What's he saying?' whispered Polly to Miasma.

Miasma passed her silver hand over the window. The glass promptly disappeared and the two voices rose clearly from the courtyard.

'Hector McTruncheon!' cried Osbert Codseye. 'Cousin Hector! How splendid to see you after all these years!'

'No more than it is to see you, dear boy,' replied Hector McTruncheon. 'And now that I've retired, I intend to repeat the pleasure more than somewhat.'

Hector McTruncheon gave a low

whistle. 'Meet Sleuth,' he said. 'My old police dog. He retired with me, don't you know.'

Sleuth jumped down from the car and stood wagging his long, shaggy, black tail. 'Not your normal tracker dog,' explained Hector. 'Sleuth knows about water too. Has webbed feet, don't you know.'

He turned to the big black dog.

'Sleuth! Show cousin Osbert your feet!'

Up in the attic, everyone watched as Osbert bent down and appeared to shake the dog's paw.

'What a stroke of luck!' cried Miasma, her eyes shining. 'Now we'll be sure to find out what that nasty professor is up to!'

'Humph!' muttered Marmaduke. 'I've never heard of a dog with webbed feet. How do we know that one's not a fake too?'

'I have,' said Polly firmly. 'They're called Newfoundland dogs.'

'Because they come from there,' explained George. 'Newfoundland, that is.'

'Humph!' muttered Marmaduke again. 'Then we had better get on with our plan.'

'I know!' cried Miasma. 'At the

stroke of midnight, I'll race through the house in a white dress with no head!' She fell about laughing. 'I mean with no head in a white dress!'

'And I'll chase after you with a bloody axe and lots of chains,' cried Marmaduke.

'And I'll drop my hands as I stagger up the stairs!' shouted Miasma. 'Those ghost hunters will be so scared. They'll never come back!'

'Wait a minute!' cried Polly. 'You've just told us they're *not* ghost hunters.'

George nodded. 'The point is, what are Professor Rattlechain and Scarlet Icepick *really* doing here?'

The room was silent for a moment.

'I rather liked the idea of being an axeman, spooky-pet,' protested Marmaduke.

'All right, all right,' said Miasma. 'You can be an axeman if you want, but that can come later.'

Polly and George exchanged a wary look.

'Hold on a minute,' said George. 'I think we ought to –'

But suddenly the room was empty.

Miasma and Marmaduke had disappeared!

CHAPTER 4

'POLLY! GEORGE!' CRIED Aunt Gardenia. 'Where are you?'

Polly and George raced back down the corridor in time to see their aunt coming up the stairs towards them.

'Ah! There you are!' cried Aunt Gardenia. 'Osbert's cousin Hector has arrived and I want you to entertain Professor Rattlechain and Miss Icepick while I change for dinner!'

'But what about the rooms?' said George, suddenly remembering he had done nothing about them. Nor had Polly laid extra places at the dining-room table.

'Oh, that's all taken care of,' replied Aunt Gardenia. 'Those wonderful caterers are looking after everything!'

'What wonderful caterers?' asked Polly as if she was in a trance.

Aunt Gardenia laughed her high, silvery laugh. 'Oh, you know the ones,' she said. 'That sweet husband and wife team who arrived once before.'

Aunt Gardenia opened the door to her room. 'I can't say I remember their names, but they do look strangely familiar.'

Aunt Gardenia turned and smiled her little smile. 'Now, do run along. We mustn't appear rude to our guests.'

The door shut behind her.

'Those wonderful caterers,' muttered Polly.

'That sweet husband and wife team,' replied George in a hollow voice.

'Oh no!' they said together.

Because Polly and George could remember very clearly what had happened the first time Marmaduke and Miasma had come downstairs to help run Creakie Hall. It had been the night the hotel inspectors arrived and what with Miasma's frogspawn cocktails and Marmaduke's roast sparrows, it became very clear indeed that the ghostly ancestors' idea of catering was extremely unusual, to put it mildly.

Polly and George walked silently down the stairs, each lost in their own memories.

Just as they turned the last flight, Polly put a warning hand on George's shoulder. She held a finger to her lips and pointed.

Below them in the front hall, stood Professor Swindel Rattlechain and his assistant, Scarlet Icepick.

They were standing in front of the portraits of Miasma and Marmaduke, staring at them as if they could see something special in them.

'I'd say these are the ones,' said Professor Rattlechain in a harsh rasping voice.

Beside him, Scarlet Icepick smiled a small mean smile. 'No doubt about it,' she replied.

Polly and George froze.

What if Miasma and Marmaduke were wrong after all?

What if these two nasty people really *could* track down ghosts with their foul whirring machine?

But worst of all, what could be done about it now?

At that moment Professor

Rattlechain looked round. 'Good evening,' he said, quickly turning his back on the portraits. 'You must be Polly and George.'

'Your aunt has told us all about you,' said Scarlet Icepick. She smiled like a weasel. 'You have a lovely place here.'

'I hope your rooms are comfortable,' said George coldly.

'Quite satisfactory, thank you,' replied Swindel Rattlechain. 'I especially liked the lacy gold cobwebs in the corners.'

'I had silver ones in my room,' said Scarlet Icepick. 'And one of them had a big woolly spider knitted in the middle of it.' She laughed. 'And do you know, its eyes seemed to follow you all around the room.'

'I suppose they want to keep an eye on us, dear,' said Swindel

Rattlechain with a thin smile. 'Some people still think our profession is slightly strange. Suspicious even.'

For a moment, Polly forgot all about Miasma's eccentric ideas about decoration. These people could sleep on a bed of nails for all she cared. She stared at his smile and the hard eyes that glittered like chips of shiny black rock behind his gold glasses.

Whatever he was, this man was not a professor of anything. She was sure of it.

'Excuse me, ladies and gentlemen.' Marmaduke strode into the hall. He was dressed in the black jacket and trousers and white-collared shirt of a butler. An enormous corkscrew hung from his lapel like a watch chain.

Polly and George watched in amazement as he picked up a wooden beater and bashed a huge brass dinner gong that had suddenly appeared outside the dining-room door.

The hall resounded with a tremendous *bonging* noise.

'Gracious!' cried Aunt Gardenia, coming down the stairs in a rustle of pink organza. 'How splendid! A dinner gong! Now, who are we still waiting for?'

At that moment, Osbert Codseye and Hector McTruncheon walked in the front door with Sleuth at their heels.

'My apologies for any delay, dear lady,' said Hector McTruncheon. 'Osbert has been giving us the, ah, guided tour, don't you know.'

'Excellent,' cried Aunt Gardenia, oblivious of the fact that Polly and George were glaring at Professor Rattlechain and Scarlet Icepick, that Osbert and Hector had ignored them completely and that Sleuth had started to growl.

'Shall we go through?' cried Aunt Gardenia. And like a ship in full sail, she surged into the dining room.

It was immediately obvious to Polly and George that Marmaduke and Miasma's ideas on catering had not changed much from the roast sparrows and frogspawn cocktails, although at least this time there were no smoking spits and certainly not a trace of straw on the floor.

The dining-room table glittered with crystal and silver all laid out on a long snowy damask cloth. So far so good.

Then Polly's eyes travelled across the room.

A huge buffet was arranged on a sideboard. There were salads and vegetables of all kinds. In the middle sat an enormous salmon. The only thing was that all the salads and all the vegetables seemed to have eyes that followed you round the room. And the salmon had a meat cleaver sticking out of its head.

'Gracious!' murmured Aunt Gardenia. 'How quaint!'

'Food and drama!' cried Miasma, leaping into the centre of the room, dressed in white baggy trousers, a waistcoat embroidered with pearls, and a floppy chef's hat. 'It's the new concept in eating!'

'And could one ask what that concept might be?' asked Professor Rattlechain with a smug smile.

'Of course you can,' cried Miasma with her wolfish grin. She pointed to the sideboard. 'Tonight, it's "Watch Out or You'll Get It in the Neck".'

'How peculiar,' murmured Aunt Gardenia, sweetly.

'Why, thank you,' replied Miasma. 'I made it up myself. Do sit down. There are little cards in front of each chair.'

Miasma turned and beamed at Hector McTruncheon. 'And I've cooked a special bone for Sleuth.' She pointed to a huge meaty lump, sitting on a gold-edged plate at the end of the table. 'That's his place, there.'

When everyone had sat down, Miasma picked up a plate, spun it on the end of her finger and fixed Professor Rattlechain with her blazing green eyes.

'Help yourself, dear professor,' cried Aunt Gardenia in her high tinkling voice.

'Something fishy, perhaps?' suggested Miasma, brightly.

Swindel Rattlechain stood up. 'Why, thank you,' he replied. 'How very kind of you to offer.'

When everyone had been served, Polly found herself staring helplessly at her plate. She had been seated between Hector McTruncheon and Swindel Rattlechain. But no matter how hard she tried to speak, the words stuck in her mouth.

Across the table, George looked at her curiously. Polly wondered if her face was white or perhaps it was bright red. At any rate, the longer she sat next to Professor Rattlechain, the more uncomfortable she felt.

Suddenly the professor put his knife and fork together on his plate. As he pushed his chair away from the table, his napkin fell on to the floor and he reached to pick it up.

Polly watched in slow motion as the sleeve of his shirt rode up his arm. For a split second she found herself staring at a tattoo.

It was a picture of a broken window entwined with roses. *WHAT'S*

YOURS IS MINE was written in wavy letters around it.

The so-called Professor Rattlechain was a thief!

Amidst the murmur of conversation and the scrape of knives on china, Polly heard the professor's harsh rasping voice. 'If you'll excuse us, Aunt Gardenia. Miss Icepick and I will retire.' He bowed and turned towards the door. 'As you know, we have a busy evening in front of us.'

'Of course, dear professor,' cried Aunt Gardenia. 'Feel free to do what you think best.'

Polly felt her head was going to explode. She stared desperately at George but he was talking to Osbert Codseye. What's worse, Miasma and Marmaduke had disappeared so she couldn't warn them either!

Polly felt trapped in her chair as surely as if she were tied to it.

'Is something the matter, dear?' asked Hector McTruncheon on her other side. 'You look a bit unwell.'

Polly turned and looked into Hector McTruncheon's kind, whiskery face. Of course! Hector McTruncheon was an ex-policeman, he'd know what to do!

A huge wave of relief washed over her.

She opened her mouth to speak. But somehow, it had all been too much and Hector McTruncheon only just managed to catch her as she slumped off her chair in a faint!

Chapter 5

Polly opened her eyes to a kaleidoscope of faces above her.

'Poor darling!' cried Aunt Gardenia, waving a lacy handkerchief smelling strongly of lavender under her nose. 'Whatever is the matter?'

Polly stared at the faces. She wondered how long she had fainted for. She looked around. She was still in the dining room.

George helped her to a chair.

'George,' gasped Polly, grabbing his arm, 'they're thieves! They're not ghost hunters. They're thieves!'

'What on earth are you talking about, dear?' asked Aunt Gardenia. 'Try this one.' She pulled another handkerchief out of her sleeve. This one smelled strongly of eucalyptus.

Polly coughed and spluttered and pushed the handkerchief away. 'Aunt Gardenia!' she cried. 'Those people are thieves. We must stop them before it's too late.'

'I beg your pardon?' cried Aunt Gardenia. Her tiny hands clutched nervously at the pink frills of her evening dress.

Hector McTruncheon cleared his throat. 'If you will excuse me, ma'am,'

he said in a serious voice. 'I must say, as a former policeman, I too find Professor Rattlechain and his assistant, Miss Scarlet Icepick, very suspicious indeed.' Hector McTruncheon rocked back on his heels. 'And so, might I add, does Sleuth, my dog.'

Aunt Gardenia's eyes sparkled with irritation. It was the first time George had ever seen her look cross. 'Is that so, Mr McTruncheon?' she said crisply. 'Well, perhaps we had better speak to them ourselves.'

With that, Aunt Gardenia drew herself up and proceeded through the dining-room door like a wedding cake on wheels.

A second later there was a shriek.

Osbert Codseye rushed forward and was just in time to catch Aunt Gardenia as she fell towards the floor in a heap of crumpled organza!

Polly and George ran into the front hall. At first they couldn't see what was wrong. Then suddenly their eyes were drawn to the wall where the portraits of Marmaduke and Miasma always hung.

In front of them were two full-length blank spaces.

The portraits had gone!

Polly rushed to the front door and pulled it open. The black bullet-shaped van wasn't there either.

'They've gone!' she sobbed. 'And they've taken the portraits with them!' Tears welled up in her eyes and began to drip down her cheeks. 'We'll never catch them now!'

'Oh yes we will, young Polly!'

said Hector McTruncheon, pulling a blanket-sized handkerchief out of his pocket and handing it to her. 'You see, I've had my suspicions for some time now, ever since I set eyes on the scoundrels, in fact.'

He turned and patted his dog's broad, curly-haired head. 'So earlier this evening, Sleuth and I took the precaution of locking the front gate.'

'But what about the iron fence around the grounds?' cried George. 'They'll climb over it.'

'No, they won't,' said a low voice. Osbert Codseye appeared from the study where he had laid Aunt Gardenia on the flowery sofa. 'I electrified it earlier this evening and I've switched it on this minute.'

George gasped. 'You mean Creakie Hall is surrounded by an electric fence?'

Osbert Codseye nodded and, for the second time, a big grin spread slowly across his face. 'And don't forget the gates have spikes on top.'

'So you see, dear children,' said Hector McTruncheon, 'we can all go to bed and sort things out tomorrow.'

As he spoke, he looked at the pocket watch that hung from his waistcoat. 'Goodness, it's almost midnight!'

'Almost midnight!' cried Polly and George.

If Miasma and Marmaduke showed up now as the headless woman chased by the clanking axeman, everything would be ruined!

George grabbed Polly's arm and turned to the two startled-looking grown-ups in the hall.

'You're right! It's way past our bedtime,' he shouted.

And without another word, the two

of them raced up the stairs as fast as they could.

Hector McTruncheon shook his head. 'Kids,' he muttered. 'We'll never understand 'em. Will we, Sleuth?'

As Polly and George turned down the long corridor, they saw Miasma and Marmaduke coming towards them.

At least, they hoped it was Miasma and Marmaduke. A headless woman in a long white dress was sauntering down the hall, chatting to a masked man waving an axe. Or rather the head tucked underneath the white-sleeved arm was chatting.

'Greetings, flesh'n'bloods,' cried Miasma. 'Polly dear, you must look at me when I talk to you!'

'Your head, spooky-pet, your head,' explained Marmaduke. 'Put it back on your shoulders. Poor Polly doesn't know where to look.'

'Oh dear,' muttered Miasma. 'I'm sorry, Polly. I hope I didn't upset you.'

Polly swallowed and fought back her tears. 'No, no, it's not that, it's —'

'Quite right,' said Miasma, putting her head on backwards. 'It's the details that matter, isn't it, bogey-baby?'

'It is, it is,' cried Marmaduke, turning her head so it faced in the right direction.

'Marmaduke, Miasma,' said George in a gruff voice. He paused because he knew what he had to say would upset them. 'The thing is, well, a terrible thing has happened.'

Marmaduke's dark eyes glowed in his head. It was as if he were reading George's mind. He turned and walked back down the corridor.

'But ghosty-kins,' wailed Miasma, 'what about our appearance at the appointed hour? I've been practising all evening!'

Marmaduke looked hard at Miasma.

It didn't take Miasma long. Marmaduke's eyes told her everything. 'Oh no,' she moaned, clasping an icy hand to her silver brow. 'What are we going to do now?'

Marmaduke took charge. 'We're going back to the attic,' he said firmly. 'And we're going to make a plan.'

CHAPTER 6

'SO YOU SEE,' said George finally as they all sat in a circle by the attic window. 'It's not as bad as it seems. They are trapped in the grounds. We just have to find them.'

Polly was sitting cross-legged in a big leather chair. 'The only problem is that it's dark,' she said.

'That's not a problem, flesh'n'blood,' cried Miasma, patting her knee kindly. 'There's a full moon and leopards can see in the dark.'

Marmaduke grinned. 'So can giant vampire bats!'

'Spooky-pet!' said Miasma, sternly. 'There's no such thing as a giant *vampire* bat.'

'All right, all right,' muttered Marmaduke, who could feel his control of the situation slipping away. 'What about a giant ordinary bat, then?'

'What about it?' asked George, looking completely mystified. 'What's it got to do with finding Professor Rattlechain and Scarlet Icepick and your portraits?'

'Everything!' cried Miasma, clapping her hands happily. 'Marmaduke, we'll have an adventure yet!'

Now Marmaduke's eyes were sparkling and his arms were making strange flapping movements. 'This is the plan,' he said in a voice that had gone all squeaky. 'You two, dear things, go to bed and have a nice long sleep.'

'And don't worry about anything,' said Miasma, passing her hand gently in front of them.

The next moment, Polly yawned and to her surprise turned over in her own bed and went back to sleep.

Beside her, George dreamt that he was sleepwalking down the stairs from the attic into his own room. It was a strange dream, sort of back to front. George stretched and put his hands behind his head and fell into a deep sleep.

'Betcha I find 'em first!' cried Miasma as she leapt from the window. Her yellow leopard's eyes glinted in the moonlight.

'Betcha you don't!' squeaked Marmaduke, flapping his huge skinny wings and heading off into the night.

Miasma landed with a soft thud on the ground and padded off into the bushes.

She didn't see Osbert Codseye taking a last breath of fresh air before going to bed.

There was a soft *thud* as Osbert

Codseye fell to his knees and tumbled onto the ground.

'Knock me down with a feather!' exclaimed Hector McTruncheon when Sleuth led him to Osbert Codseye's slumped body. 'Sleuth, dear boy, there's more than meets the eye going on here.'

At that moment, a huge bat flapped over his head, circled the house once and flew away towards the lake. Hector McTruncheon stayed calm. After all, he hadn't spent fifty years in the police force for nothing. He closed his eyes and opened them again.

When the bat disappeared, Hector McTruncheon dragged his cousin across the gravel and into the front hall. Then, with a hand that shook like a pneumatic drill, he poured himself a nightcap that came to the top of a pint mug.

Miasma found Professor Rattlechain's van in the woods. It was easy for a leopard – all you had to do was follow the nasty, sweet smell of thieves.

Miasma rested her huge paws on the tinted window and peered inside.

The back of Scarlet Icepick's shaved blonde hair was in front of her. Opposite her sat a sharp-faced man with rings in his ears and greasy, black hair tied back in a ponytail. At first, Miasma wondered if there was a third thief in the gang. Then her eyes slid to a heap on the floor. A wavy, white wig and a pair of square, gold glasses lay on top of pinstripe trousers and a frock coat.

'So, clever clogs, Professor Swindel Rattlechain,' sneered Scarlet Icepick. 'What are we going to do now? We're locked in.'

'Shaddup an'I'll think of something!' shouted Professor Rattlechain whose real name was Eddie Link. (And whose real business was robbing whatever old house he could con himself into.)

At that moment, Marmaduke landed on Miasma's shoulders. 'I've looked everywhere for our portraits,' he squeaked. 'I can't see them anywhere.' He pressed his bat's pug-nose against the van's tinted-glass window. 'Are they in here?'

Miasma growled under her breath. 'Maybe it's time we asked.'

Scarlet Icepick jumped up. 'Eddie!' she said in a hoarse whisper. 'Did you hear that? It sounds as if there's a leopard out there.'

Eddie Link stared through the tinted window. His face went grey and the rings in his ears began to rattle. 'There is,' he said in a low voice. 'And there's a giant bat sitting on its shoulder.'

'I think you're seeing things,' said Scarlet slowly but without turning round. 'But, um, I think it's a sign we're in the wrong place, Eddie.'

Even though Scarlet Icepick was as much a thief as her partner, all this business about hunting ghosts had begun to make her nervous.

'Eddie,' she said again. 'It's those portraits. We shouldn't have nicked 'em.'

Eddie Link's mouth went up and down but no words came out.

On the other side of the window, Miasma smiled a wide hungry smile by way of encouragement.

'Eddie!' shouted Scarlet Icepick, as she kicked him on the knee with her black boots. 'Say something!'

But Eddie Link had passed out and lay in a heap on top of Professor Rattlechain's pinstripe trousers.

Scarlet Icepick climbed into the driver's seat. There was only one thing to do and it looked like she was going to have to do it on her own. It was as if she were under a strange spell.

She drove slowly out of the woods, down the drive and round to Osbert Codseye's garden shed.

One by one, she picked up the portraits that she and Eddie had hidden underneath some fertiliser sacks and carried them into the front hall. Somehow (later, she didn't know *how* at all), she lifted them both onto the wall.

Then she dumped Eddie Link on to the gravel outside Creakie Hall and rolled the black bullet-shaped van into Bullfrog Lake.

When Eddie finally came to, the moon had faded with the first light of dawn. The strangest dream was still in his head. He saw himself and Scarlet Icepick walking up the long gravel drive towards a pair of tall iron gates.

The shadow of a giant bat fluttered on the white gravel in front of them. A huge black leopard with gleaming pointed teeth walked silently behind them.

Eddie opened his eyes and his knees turned to jelly.

It hadn't been a dream. He *was* standing at the gates and they were swinging open in front of them.

'Come on,' croaked Scarlet Icepick, grabbing Eddie by the arm. 'Let's get out of this place.'

As they stumbled onto the road, the gates of Creakie Hall clanged together with a hollow ghostly sound that echoed through the still morning air.

The next morning, Sleuth stood dripping in the front hall. He wore square, gold glasses and something white and hairy hung from his mouth.

'Gracious!' cried Aunt Gardenia, who was still feeling a little dazed after the events of the previous night. 'What on earth is that, Mr McTruncheon? And why is that dog wearing glasses?'

'It's a wig, ma'am,' replied Hector McTruncheon. 'And I must inform you that my inquiries reveal that Professor Rattlechain and his assistant were nothing better than common burglars. As for the glasses . . .' Hector McTruncheon's voice faded away.

'But the portraits, Mr McTruncheon,' cried Aunt Gardenia. 'Who returned the portraits?'

Hector McTruncheon stared at his feet. 'That we'll never know,' he replied, thinking vaguely of the huge bat that he had pretended not to see the night before. 'Perhaps there *are* ghosts in Creakie Hall, after all.'

'Nonsense, Mr McTruncheon,' laughed Aunt Gardenia. 'I'm sure there's a perfectly good explanation.' She disappeared into her study. 'It's just that we've somehow forgotten it.'

Hector McTruncheon bent down. He removed the gold glasses and took the white-haired wig from Sleuth's mouth. 'Sleuth, old boy,' he whispered, 'I'll never forget that bat for the rest of my life.'

The hall was empty by the time Polly and George came sleepily down the stairs. All night they had had the strangest dreams about bats and leopards and big iron gates.

The first thing they saw were the portraits of Miasma and Marmaduke Bogey-Mandeville.

'George!' gasped Polly. 'They're back!'

For a moment neither of them spoke. Then Polly and George burst out laughing.

In the pictures, a tiny blood-stained axe hung like a jewel from Marmaduke's belt. While beside him, Miasma was cradling a little doll in a white dress. The funny thing was its head was tucked underneath its arm!